RIDICULOUS WRITERS

Fictional Fun

Edited By Jenni Harrison

First published in Great Britain in 2020 by:

Young Writers
Remus House
Coltsfoot Drive
Peterborough
PE2 9BF
Telephone: 01733 890066
Website: www.youngwriters.co.uk

Printed and bound in the UK by BookPrintingUK
Website: www.bookprintinguk.com
YB0447G

FOREWORD

Ladies and gentlemen, boys and girls, roll up roll
up to see the weirdest and wackiest creations
the world of fiction has ever seen!

Young Writers presents to you the wonderful results of
Ridiculous Writers, our latest competition for primary
school pupils. We gave them the task of creating a crazy
combo to give them a character or an object around which
they could base their story. They picked an adjective or
verb and a noun at random and the result is some super
creations, along with the added bonus of reinforcing
their grammar skills in a fun and engaging way.

But the fun didn't end there, oh no! Once they had
their subject they had to write a story, with the added
challenge of doing it in just **100 words!** I think you'll
agree they've achieved that brilliantly – this book is
jam-packed with wacky and wonderful tales.

Here at Young Writers we want to pass our love of the written
word onto the next generation and what better way to do that
than to celebrate their writing by publishing it in a book! We
believe their confidence and love of creative writing will grow,
and hopefully these young writers will one day be the authors
of the future. An absorbing insight into the imagination of the
young, we hope you will agree that this amazing anthology
is one to delight the whole family again and again.

CONTENTS

Joshua Harvey Bensley (9) 48
Grace Wheatley (10) 49
Evelyn Fordham 50
Lily Smith (8) 51
Max Norris (8) 52
Theo Kamm (9) 53
Kian Marsh (9) 54
Imogen Francesca Darley (10) 55
Macey Smith (8) 56
Stephanie Gregson (7) 57
Rupert Gregson (10) 58
Alex Brennan (10) 59
Sid-John Holland (8) 60
Charlie Marwood (9) 61
Lewis Elvidge (8) 62
Oliver Fordham (9) 63
Byron Aston-Ottey (9) 64

Grange Park Primary School, Winchmore Hill

Gabriel Mansbridge (9) 65
Francesca Koceku (10) 66
Reggie Perkins (10) 67
Mira Cosgun (10) 68
Jing-Yang Koh (9) 69
David McMillan-Ward (9) 70
Vaanika Bhatt (9) 71
Isabel Minguez (9) 72
Kristiano Pugliese (9) 73
Lara Zachoria (10) 74
G-J Ohi Wahid (9) 75
Sofia Bernstein (10) 76
Alexander Antoniou (10) 77
Sam Alimohammadi (10) 78
Hugh Murphy (10) 79
Yunus Coskun (10) 80
Ollie Bannister (10) 81
Ikram Mohamed (9) 82
Samuel Gonzales (10) 83
Arseniy Ermolovich (10) 84
Nihar Vaidya (9) 85
Havin Uludag (9) 86

Holy Trinity CE Primary School, Seaton Carew

Charlie Jardine (8) 87
Dougie (7) 88
Connie Carlton (8) 89
Isla Sutton (8) 90

Kingsteignton School, Kingsteignton

Natalia Hanuscakova (9) 91
Noah Gibbs (9) 92
Rosie Burns (8) 93

Millbrook Community Primary School, Kirkby

Sienna Pike (8) 94
Lexie Mae Howard (10) 95
Annie Browne (9) 96
Lacey Sayer (9) 97
Aimee Price (9) 98
Riley Brognoli-Vinten (9) 99
Harry Daulby (9) 100
Ethan Lundon (9) 101
Ella Hughes (9) 102
Jacob Fisher (9) 103
Ethan Riley (9) 104
Nicholas McCarthy (10) 105
Clensy (8) 106
Elizabeth Lewis (9) 107
Phoebe Gibbs (9) 108
Ria McVerry (8) 109
Sadie Walsh (10) 110

Roach Vale Primary School, Colchester

Matilda-Rose Labdon (7) 111
Alana Lawrence-Skinner (8) 112
Sophie Enever (10) 113
Annabelle Richardson (7) 114
Jessica Day (8) 115
Poppy Ella-Rose Goodchild (8) 116

Stella Wegrzanowska (8)	117
Sophie Dale (8)	118
Gracie Topolewski (7)	119
Kash Weightman (8)	120
Amelia Smith (8)	121
Harry Holding (8)	122
Lola Mann (7)	123
Evie Tuttlebee (7)	124
Jude Phillips (7)	125
Reggie Morrisson (8)	126
Joshua Partridge (8)	127
Lily Woodhouse (8)	128

South Malling CE Primary School, Lewes

Beth Walden (8)	129
Jenson Beal (7)	130

St Andrew's CE Junior School, Burnham-On-Sea

Adam Herniman (9)	131

St Chad's RC Primary School, South Norwood

Grace Tshimuna (8)	132
Michelle Appiah Arhin (9)	133
Kayla Mcdermoth (10)	134
Nwabueze Akubueze (10)	135
Rosalee Edwards (11)	136
Dara Ukhun (11)	137
Tiffany Nheta (10)	138
Amenan Yao (8)	139

St John Fisher Primary School, Littlemore

Sienna Carbon (9)	140
Cameron Lewis (9)	141
Filip Sypniewski (7)	142
Imogen Meek (9)	143

St Stephen's Community Academy, Launceston

Nataly Masi (9)	144
Tyler Jasper (8)	145
Harry Lancaster (8)	146
Megan Laugharne (8)	147

Temple Ewell CE Primary School, Temple Ewell

Joshua Waller (9)	148
Poppy Wallace (9)	150
Harry Pettet (8)	151
Alf Player (9)	152
Lauren Stokes (10)	153
Chloe Leach (10)	154
Sophia Harper Wight (9)	155
Dylan Chalmers (10)	156
Lotte Buckman (9)	157
Alessio Del Duca (9)	158
Jude Magdalena (10)	159
Kesnia-Bry Bunting (10)	160
Hope Jordan (9)	161
Georgie Readings (9)	162
Harry Chambers (9)	163
Tyler Browne (9)	164

Winkleigh Primary School, Winkleigh

Elanor Florence Spillett Smith (11)	165
Gracie Goddard (11)	166
Rosanna Clark (11)	167
Charlotte Ellicott (10)	168

Wood Farm Primary School, Headington

Liana Roopesh (10)	169
Ayman Saadi Mahir (9)	170
Klaudia Stawinska (10)	171
Hamdi Guled Guled Hasan (10)	172
Nadine Da Silva (9)	173

THE STORIES

Gerald Giraffe

Gerald giraffe was hungry. "Go and eat some leaves," said his mum. Gerald loved leaves, but struggled to stretch his neck high enough.
I'll find a small tree, thought Gerald. He walked and walked, but no small tree was in sight. The only leaves were up high, so Gerald stretched his neck higher and higher, but still couldn't reach. Gerald was sad. "What's up?" said Maisy Monkey. "I can't reach any leaves." sobbed Gerald. Maisy Monkey wanted to help, so she hung off a branch and handed leaves down into Gerald's mouth. This made Gerald very, very, very happy again.

Sydney Thorpe (8)
Bishop Alexander Academy, Newark

The Gangsta Ninja

The raven sky enclosed the bustling city of London. From the shadows, a mysterious figure leapt across rooftops. Wearing glamorous sapphire robes, he dived onto the rooftop of the bank. What was he doing? Without warning, he punched through glass, landing on luxurious marble floor. Checking his surroundings, he found what he was looking for. The vault door. He threw a grenade at it, revealing stacks of cash. He grabbed the money and turned to see a policeman. He touched his necromancer ring, which sent shadows hurling at him. But there was more to come, this was just the beginning...

Harry Clarke (11)
Bishop Alexander Academy, Newark

The Crazy Pizza

One day the crazy pizza had a dream of going on holiday on the beach. The crazy pizza went on holiday. She met Ketchup on the plane, so they went on holiday together.

When they got to the beach, the pizza smelt nice. The people wanted to eat her. She went to Ketchup and shouted, "Help!"

Ketchup said, "Okay." He started squirting at the people. They went away. Pizza and Ketchup became best friends and lived together in Pizzaburg. They met more friends and had lots of fun at the party with many other friends. They lived happily ever after.

Julia Wojkowska (9)
Bishop Alexander Academy, Newark

3

The Hungry Ninja

So at the dead of night, Hungry Ninja snuck out of his house to meet Dumpster Diving Dude because they were starving. They had such a feast. There were eggshells, Cheestrings, spaghetti, gherkin. They even had the entire Milky Way, Mars... Okay, maybe I was exaggerating. Maybe just a Milky Way and a Mars bar.

But one night, things weren't right. There was a whole chicken laid out. They thought nothing of it until they got caught in a blanket and never ever, ever returned. But who did it? Who dared to do such a scheme? *Dun, dun, dun...*

Finley Eteo (11)
Bishop Alexander Academy, Newark

Where Did She Go?

After years of pain from those insufferable bullies, who one by one were draining the life out of me. Who am I? Bethany Armstrong. "Argh!" I suddenly disappeared into the unknown. I felt adrenaline surge through my body; I became Bloodshot, the evil superhero. I was wearing dishevelled black-like doom rags. Was I helping these bullies or was I fighting evil in my antiquated mind? What should I do? All of a sudden, I felt light-headed, but the more I moved, the worse it got. Then I felt myself falling with silence all around me; I felt my...

Evie Harris (11)
Bishop Alexander Academy, Newark

The Strawberry And The Salad Bowl

Strawberry woke up and it was the big day. It was her competition of the year called The Fruit Bowl. She looked over at the clock and realised it was 7.45am, when she had to get ready. When she finished, she reached out for her pink bow. It wasn't there. Where was it? She couldn't find her bow. It was almost time to go. Luckily, Banana her boyfriend came over and found it.

They were at the competition and he cheered when she scored a high score. They finished all the challenges and Strawberry's team won! Banana was so proud!

Kayla Baillie (11)
Bishop Alexander Academy, Newark

The Girl Who Got Evacuated

One day Lilly woke up to go to school until everything changed. At 12am in the morning, her and her friends sat down to eat her rationed lunch. Then that was where it all changed. There were alarms going off, people rushing out of the school. Then they got on the train, but some people couldn't go to different homes because their family weren't as fortunate as others. So some children got left behind. Lilly and her friends were in the same village. They still had homes back home where they were more at risk of getting injured badly.

Lola Booth (11)
Bishop Alexander Academy, Newark

The Burping And Trumping Toilet

Have you ever wondered if toilets can eat you? This is why you shouldn't stay on the toilet for a long time...

Freddie ran desperately to the toilet holding his bottom. He looked at the rainbow toilet and the toilet looked back at him. He was on there for too long. It was too late! The toilet quickly and greedily ate him up! Suddenly, the toilet was jumping up and down and he burped Freddie out! That was the moment when Freddie decided that he'd never sit on the toilet again. He wore nappies again, even though he was ten.

Millie Toomer (8)
Bishop Alexander Academy, Newark

Naughty Doctor

It was just an ordinary morning until... Doctor got bitten. She was bitten by a mysterious, blue, venomous snake. It made her feel strange, so she got in her car and left for work. She worked at the doctors with her best friend Chloe. Chloe noticed the doctor's eyes were red not blue. Doctor started to fight Chloe. She had turned evil. Chloe made a magical potion made from flowers, fruit and fairy dust. She put it in the freezer, then told Doctor it was an ice lolly. She ate it, but it made her disappear. Where had she gone?

Layla Clarke (8)
Bishop Alexander Academy, Newark

The Crazy Scientist

The crazy scientist made a portal to a molten lava dimension to rule mighty Washington. He sent Lava Monster to break the city to rule it! No one could stop him, but the monster stopped listening to him and he got sent to the different dimension with lava. He kept trying to get out, but it did not work. So he made a new invention to get out and it worked! He got out and destroyed the portal so the city was safe. People had to rebuild it, so they did. The scientist went to prison for very long.

Filip Wojkowski (9)
Bishop Alexander Academy, Newark

Yarn-Bombed!

Mittens the cat was playing with a ball of yarn in the living room. Little did she know, the yarn was tangled everywhere! "Wow!" said Mittens' owner, "Bad cat! You yarn-bombed the living area! Out you go!" Mittens was scared. Would she kick her out forever?

Outside, Mittens found a ball of yarn. Mittens met a friend outside named Moonlight. Her and Moonlight yarn-bombed the bushes outside as well! "Uh-oh!" they miaowed. As they untangled the yarn, it felt like they were yarn-bombing all over again! Mittens' owner watched them from the window playing with a ball of yarn, not yarn-bombing!

Evie Knifton (9)
Christ Church CE Primary School, Greenwich

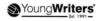

The Very Stinky Teacher!

One day there was a new teacher teaching Year 4. Everybody said she was so stinky and she was the size of Daddy Pig, but with very skinny legs. The teacher was named Miss Vong. After school, she cried and cried. She said, "Why me? Why do I have to be bullied? Everyone thinks I'm a pig!"
The very next day, Miss Vong heard a neighbour say, "Look at Vong, she's so stinky!"
At school, Miss Vong said to everyone, "I'm having five children and I'm allergic to water. Do you all have an issue with that? So stop it!"

Emme Walusimbi (9)
Christ Church CE Primary School, Greenwich

Clumsy Monster

One day there was a monster called Dirty. He did not like celebrating and he was clumsy. He didn't pick up his own clothes and he didn't even bother to wash them.

Another day, Dirty wasn't looking forward to a party. So he had a shower, got dressed and then he went to the party. But everyone was looking at him because he wasn't wearing his pants. So he had to run home and put his pants back on. Then he went back to the party, but he didn't have a friend. Then a girl said, "Want to be friends?"

Hollie Pethers (9)
Christ Church CE Primary School, Greenwich

The Naughty Superhero And The Mad Scientist

There is this naughty superhero that pushes banks and other important buildings down. He steals the money and he goes all over the world to buy things. But there is this mad scientist that is always following him who knows how to reduce his power and take it away. But he is always moving, he never stops. He has a super boy and that boy likes rats and squirrels. He can shape-shift into different animals, but finally he aims and fires. He finally gets him. He catches him quickly and takes him to jail. Everyone's happy.

Kobby Adomako (9)
Christ Church CE Primary School, Greenwich

The Talking Clothes!

There was once a boy named Alex who was ten years old. He was very clever and loved going to school. That day was his first scary day of his new school. He was getting dressed to go to school when he heard something. "Hi Alex!" it said. He looked around and did not see anyone. So he just went to school and acted like nothing happened. During class, he asked the teacher if he could go to the toilet. Alex did not go to the toilet, instead he said hi to himself and knew it was his clothes.

Riyam Banitorfi (9)
Christ Church CE Primary School, Greenwich

The Burping Pirate

Long ago, a burping pirate burped his way off a plank. This is how the story went. A long time ago, pirates gathered on a boat to find a treasure chest so they could be rich, but one of the pirates found the treasure and kept it all to himself. Two of the pirates found out about it and all of them gathered up and made a plan to make the burping pirate walk off the plank, for burping revenge. The next day, the pirates woke up the traitor and he burped his butt away forever.

Amelia Ekeke (9)
Christ Church CE Primary School, Greenwich

The Killer

As the terrifying chef sliced off another head, many people started to lose their lives. People were stood still, they couldn't move. They were frozen in fear! As his worst enemy stormed in, he shuddered. He couldn't move. He tried to, but he couldn't move an inch. As his enemy moved closer and closer to him, he grabbed the blood-dripping knife from his bare, shaking hands. *Slice!* He was no longer alive. Crowds and crowds of people rose up and cheered. It was like a festival. The terrifying chef was defeated at last. The smiles of people grew.

Chloe James (10)
Coton Green Primary School, Tamworth

The Evil Football

A clumsy young boy called Wobble woke up one day and wanted to play football with his dad. His dad explained that they were going to climb Mount Everest. On his way out, he tripped over the doorstep. Then they suddenly arrived on a crazy football pitch on top of Mount Everest. Him and his dad played football. Wobble kept missing all his shots. He took another shot, but it bounced back. His dad thought he was being his clumsy self, but then his dad realised it was the ball. So they went home and called it the Evil Football!

Jamie Ealing-Bowe (10)
Coton Green Primary School, Tamworth

Trumping Brother

My brother Lukas was obsessed with eating beans. Every day he had them in the garden on his deckchair. Whenever he swallowed them, his belly bloated and then released a really smelly fart. He went to school and every day he got sent home because of the farting.

One night, before he went to sleep he ate more beans. He woke up and did a ridiculously loud, smelly fart which woke everyone up. He then did a loud rumble. Green gas shot out of his bum and he zoomed up into space and landed on the International Space Centre.

Isabel Howard (9)

Coton Green Primary School, Tamworth

The Wrath Of The Pepperoni Pizza

Once there was a man who ordered a pepperoni pizza. He dropped a piece without realising. The pizza slice sat there for years, until one day it got so stinky it came to life. It walked to the door to get revenge for being left. It went out and after ages of being free, the world smelt like mouldy cheese, stale dough and gooey pepperoni. Everyone hated the smell so much, they left the Earth and went to the moon. The pizza was not sad because the people that were left became his slaves and he ruled the entire world!

Daisy Green (11)
Coton Green Primary School, Tamworth

The Unicorn Who Just Wants Friends

Up in Cloud Kingdom, there was a unicorn, The Annoying Unicorn to be precise. She went to Unicorn School with all her unicorn friends. Well, she would if she had friends. She went to try and talk to Shy Unicorn at break, but she walked away. Then she tried Loud Unicorn, he walked away too. When Annoying Unicorn had given up, Kind Unicorn came and spoke to her. Kind Unicorn said, "I don't think you're annoying, do you want to be friends?" Annoying Unicorn was happy, she had a friend now. That's how she finally became the Not Annoying Unicorn.

Jasmine Louise Ward (11)

Elland CE Primary School, Elland

The Naughty Pizza

Once there was a naughty pizza who was no Pepperoni, simply a Margherita. Slowly he was pulled out of a fire, he couldn't believe his eyes... KIDS!

His sister Americana was brutally murdered by these creatures. A plump boy picked up the pizza, but Margherita jolted out of the boy's hands, fleeing. That was the work of the devil. Boasting - he escaped.

Years later, Margherita arrived at the restaurant. A waiter came and asked if he wanted a drink. "I'll have a Margarita, the cocktail," said Margherita. "Cannibal," replied the waiter. Then Margherita saw a plump gentleman - DEATH WAS NEAR!

Matthew Oliver Monehen (10)
English Martyrs Catholic Primary School, London

The Lazy Monster

"Urgh! Who would want to do this assessment about planets? Who would care about going to Neptune?" groaned Sebi miserably. So he sat on the sofa watching television, when the most amazing thing happened...

It turned into a portal which transported him to Neptune! *Thud!* "What on Mars?" Sebi asked.

Just five minutes later, he was already having the time of his life at a fantastic disco with the guppies!

Three hours later, the guppies sent him on a rocket back to ordinary Mars! Inspired, Sebi sat down to write his assessment, which would win him a trip to... Neptune!

Katerina Corossi (10)
English Martyrs Catholic Primary School, London

Dr Burp's Fizziest Drink

Dr Burgeon wanted to create the fizziest drink ever. He drank so many that he was nicknamed Burp. He needed the best ingredients in the universe. He needed golden lemons from Atlantis and cream from unicorns. The final ingredient was the hardest to obtain. It was Martian berries. He had to stowaway on a spaceship to get to Mars. To get home, he burped to propel himself through space.

Back in his lab, he mixed the ingredients and tested the new drink. It was so fizzy that it made the biggest burp ever, causing pollution and the whole world ended.

Max Pasterny (11)

English Martyrs Catholic Primary School, London

The Clumsy Football

"La, la, la!" The music was playing all night long. The football knew it was his neighbour, the goalpost. All the football could hear was the loud banging from the dancing and the loud music blaring in the background. Everything stopped around 7am. The football had to leave his house or he would be fired from work. He left the house and was sleepwalking, until he bumped into a pole. The ambulance came and took the football to hospital to recover. He recovered and went home. Then the goalpost knocked on the door and said, "Sorry."

Salina Efrem (10)
English Martyrs Catholic Primary School, London

The Clumsy Rabbit

"Hello, my name's Louis." *Boing! Plafff! Boing! Plafff!* "What's that noise?" *Boing! Plafff!* "I wonder what. Look, it's a clumsy rabbit."

"Hello," said the rabbit.

"What? Wait. Let me get this straight. You're a talking clumsy rabbit, right?"

"Err, errm, yes!"

"Look! it's a dragon! Look! It's an ice gun!"

"Freeze, freeze, freeze, freeze!" *Roar!*

"Oh no, it can breathe fire!"

"I know," said Louis, "you can jump on the dragon."

"Good idea!" *Boing! Plafff!*

"Look, he's down, freeze him! Freeze!" He was in ice. "My name's Louis," said the kid.

"My name's Benjamin, bye-bye!" *Boing! Plafff! Boing!*

Samuel Rowley Otalora (7)
Europa School UK, Culham

The Rabbit That Ate All The Cakes In The World

"Wow!" said Mother Rabbit. "Peter, why are you so hungry?"

"Because you only give me veg! That never fills me up!"

"Then what do you need to fill you up?"

"I need sweets!"

"But where are you going to get the candy?"

"I will sneak into the shops."

"Peter, where will you get the-"

"Bye, Mum."

Aww, sighed Peter's mum. Whilst Peter was at the shops, he saw a cake shop. He snuck in, got a sack, got all the cakes and ate them. Then he got all the other cakes and ate them too. Finally, he went home.

Julia Atienza Miguélez (8)
Europa School UK, Culham

The Hairy Pizza

I ordered a pizza and I said, "It's a hairy pizza! I'm sure I ordered a pepperoni one!" So I called them again and said, "Can I have a pepperoni pizza?" They said, "Okay." The pizza arrived and I opened the box and said, "Another hairy pizza, this is annoying. Wait, I called the hairy pizza shop, that's why every pizza is hairy!" So I went there and asked them, "Where do you get the hair?"
They replied, "From the hairdressers, you crazy person."
"Hair is for wigs, pepperoni is for pizza. Stop making hairy pizza, stupid!"

Lucas Jones-Bauer (8)
Europa School UK, Culham

Toilet Wars: Episode I - The Toilet Menace

Finn, a former Stormtrooper, now lived a boring life. He'd just finished doing a poo, when the toilet came to life! Then it grew muscles and tried to take over the terrified world. Finn fought bravely with his darksaber. The toilet pulled out its darksaber and they fought.

Ten minutes later, the toilet had escaped and Finn needed another poo. So he did another poo in the toilet and suddenly, *ka-bam!* The toilet exploded. Finn looked down and there was a sign saying, 'Warning. Do not do two poos in this toilet or the toilet will explode.' Finn did it!

Alejandro Moshenska (7)
Europa School UK, Culham

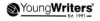

The Giant Blueberries

Once upon a time there was an evil wizard. He lived in a big castle in the middle of a dense forest. One day, the wizard had a great idea. "I shall cast a spell to make giant blueberries." So he got his spell book and flicked through the pages until he found the spell. "Make giant blueberries, so fine, so blue!" When he finished the spell, he did not notice there were blueberries in his pants!

In the forest, there lived a magical bunny and she saw the blueberries. "Make these giant blueberries disappear!" The blueberries disappeared.

Nerys Garrod (8)
Europa School UK, Culham

The Impatient Muffin

We had just got some blueberry muffins out of the oven! "So delicious," I said, "let's ice them, then leave them for tomorrow. Let's go play Monopoly." Meanwhile, in the muffin box they were getting bored. "Why? Why? Why? It is not fair! Why do pizzas get eaten straight away when they come out of the oven? I know, Barry Muffin, can you eat me?" He did, but when he came across a blueberry he would throw it to Binbel Berry Muffin who absolutely loved them. Luckily someone ate the burnt ones and that was Cherry.

Cloudagh Harding (8)
Europa School UK, Culham

The Crazy Cat

BOOM, BOOM CATY MOO! HE DID NOT LIKE PANTS! So he stopped. NO MORE PANTS FOR HIM! One day, the crazy cat stole all the pants in the galaxy. From Mars, Neptune and the other planets! There were curly pants, stripy pants, square pants and more! Weirdly, at midnight he ate all the pants, the square pants, the curly pants and much more! But he regretted it. He didn't like pants! So he stopped. No more pants for him!
So I guess that's the end of the story. The crazy cat wants to say bye. *Miaow! Miaow!* (That means bye-bye!)

Amelie Dean (8)
Europa School UK, Culham

The Teacher And Dinosaur

Once upon a time lived a teacher with a very stinky foot. All the children backed off. Then they all saw a dinosaur, so they screamed. But there was no need to scream because the dinosaur was so clumsy he destroyed all the timetable sheets. So the teacher said, "Get out of here you marshmallow tomato head, whatever you are, just get out! Outttt!"
The dinosaur started to cry and said in a dinosaur voice to the teacher, "I will never see you again!" So the dinosaur flushed the teacher down the toilet head first.

Jannah Hemamda (7)
Europa School UK, Culham

Magic Robot

A magic robot went to a creepy house. He saw a ghost hiding from him and then they met each other. They saw an English ninja who'd already chopped the robot's head off because he thought they were baddies. The robot said hello to the ninja and the ninja touched the ghost's head. The robot and the ghost said goodbye to the ninja. The robot took the ghost to his house and they played with each other. The robot said goodbye to the ghost. This made the robot cry because he missed his best friends. Then the aliens took him!

Ariadne Diaz Melgar (8)
Europa School UK, Culham

England Versus Croatia

Bang! It was a big match! England versus Croatia! The new number 10 Modric and Mason Mount were off to Russia to play the final of the World Cup. A noisy crowd were cheering for both teams: England and Croatia. It was very exciting for the fans of the two teams. Everyone shouted England x 3 and Croatia x 3. The starting eleven for Croatia was Boban in defence, Modric in midfield and the rest in attack and sub. The match was 1-0 for England, but after half-time, Croatia turned the result to 2-1 for Croatia in extra time.

Damyan Asparuhov (7)

Europa School UK, Culham

Gangster Toilet

Boom! Slap! Bang! Wallop! A man was murdered by a gangster toilet who stole all of the poor man's money, including his bank money too. The toilet was very rich. He wanted to be a golden toilet, so he needed a lot of money to afford it. *Creak!* A man was coming. Then the toilet said, "Yay! More money." It was the man's first time at this hotel and he hadn't heard of the disappearing people. So the man sat on the toilet. He left his money on his lap, but then the toilet turned gold and rich!

Oliver Goodyear (8)
Europa School UK, Culham

Muscly Super Baby And The New Galaxy

One day a super baby lived. *Kaboom!* He jumped out of his cot and flew to space through the world to a new galaxy. There was another planet full of devils and aliens they decided to attack. They had a battle. The super baby tapped a devil with his pinky finger and all of the devils and aliens died. Then the war was over. They had won. Now they owned two planets, so they built a new city on there. Everyone was having a great time, even the super baby was having the best time of his life.

Santiago Smith (7)
Europa School UK, Culham

The Evil Football!

It was on the news! The Champions League final. Liverpool vs Real Madrid. Sam, a six-year-old boy had bought tickets to the Bernabéu Stadium! In five days he would be sitting on one of the white seats! He wasn't expecting an evil football!
On the day of the match, he awoke at 5am. He was so excited! He dressed up in his Liverpool kit. At the start of the match, the ball had a mouth and bit all of the player's legs off! Sam jumped from his seat and jabbed a pin in the ball.

Ayman Parry (8)
Europa School UK, Culham

The Evil Toilet

Scribble, scribble. A gangster toilet was writing how to rule the world. The toilet went out quietly, but came face-to-face with a clumsy superhero! The hero had the help of the monster blueberries, but the toilet flushed them down. It was a vicious battle. The hero won, so he went back to his base. But the toilet popped his head out of the sewers and grinned an evil grin. "Now I will get my revenge. Hahaha... I shall destroy the superhero's base. Hahaha..."

Eloise Garrod (8)
Europa School UK, Culham

The Baby Battle

Bang! "What a big nappy," said the big baby.
"No, I want it," said the super strong baby. The two babies had a big battle. Farting in faces, throwing crazy toilets at each other! But the nappy flew off. *Kaboom!* The nappy crash-landed into little pieces. "Noooo!" said the babies. The big baby and the strong baby went crazy. They smashed and ate planets for the rest of their lives.

Louis Griffin (7)
Europa School UK, Culham

The Evil Hairy Emoji Poop

Tooott! I needed a really big poo, so I went to the toilet. I did one big poo, then I felt something ticklish. It was a hairy, evil emoji poop. I flushed it down as quickly as I could.

Then down in the sewers the emoji poop conquered the sewers. I had a boxing fight with the emoji poop. It was a terrifying battle and in the end I beat it and restored the sewers back to peace.

Bosco (8)
Europa School UK, Culham

The Hairy Pizza

Kaboom! A bang happened in space and out came... a hairy pizza! It made everything hairy! Only one hero could fix it - the stinky foot! It was so stinky no one went closer than 100 metres. They saw the stinky foot put on his jet-booster and he put the pizza in jail. Although it kept happening 100 times again.

Arthur Durkin (7)
Europa School UK, Culham

Crazy Frog Mayhem

As usual, mayhem coiled round the city and bounced through buildings while Crazy Frog rapped his ear-piercing solo, escaping the wrath of the Sensible Salamander. Unexpectedly, a trap sprung and trapped the oblivious Crazy Frog. They transported him to Sensible School, bullying him with sensible TV that paralysed him. When he broke out of his trance, Crazy Frog smashed the TV psychotically and called the Newt Nerds. They flooded Sensible School using water from the river, rescuing Crazy Frog along the way. The city returned to normal - except for Sensible School and the salamanders who were drowning in the sea.

Leo Norris (9)
Grainthorpe Junior School, Grainthorpe

Crazy Frog Jr

Crazy Frog Junior was on the toilet when the window opened suddenly. Junior ran because he was afraid. He then flew out the roof window. Junior flew over the village. The whole neighbourhood and the mayor screamed with fear. Then a chopper was after him. "Stop frog and don't move!"

"I can't stop! Help!" Then Junior got a phone call from the mayor. "Hello?" Junior said with fear. "Hello, this is the mayor, please keep the noise down!"

"Um, okay. I'll try my best, but I'm in the air right now!" He knew it would be the end maybe...

Oscar White (9)

Grainthorpe Junior School, Grainthorpe

Bubbly Farts And Jelly Poop

Throughout the silent city, rocket launches took place by the peach-sanded beach. Barry and his dog Momo volunteered to fly out to space during the apocalypse.

Just before landing, the rocket malfunctioned and fell to the moon's surface. Barry thought the men had cut some of the wires. Barry took his revenge and pooped out jelly bubbles that could suffocate millions of people! Momo helped.

Suddenly, Farting Phill arrived and shouted, "Aaarrr!" Farting Phill thankfully saved the day and farted on Barry to kill him.

As Phill returned to Earth he taught Momo how to be good.

Faith Fenwick (10)

Grainthorpe Junior School, Grainthorpe

Big Foot's Sorrow

Terrorising the town of Costarica, Sgt Bigfoot - a fraudulent, corrupted police officer, enters a rural society, having flashbacks on the atrocious things he's done... His head, slumped against a wall, seems to have shut off, who could have known what is happening! Lulling into a peculiar sleep, Sgt Bigfoot remembered his hateful life and wishes he never entered. Reminding himself how much he loved his family before the incident that was never to be spoken of again. He knows he can never pursue the life he is living in. He opens his eyes reluctantly to never be seen again...

Isaac Copley (11)
Grainthorpe Junior School, Grainthorpe

The Talking T-Shirt

One sunny day, everyone was having fun in Paris. Suddenly, a white, rude T-shirt appeared (yes, I know right!) Furiously, T-shirt said, "Ehh mate, it looks like you need a diet!" A big, fat, hairy man thought, *why can a T-shirt chat to me?* The T-shirt ran away chuckling. On its way, it met another guy, but he wasn't any kind of guy, he was a half-cow man. The half-cow man walked with T-shirt to the butcher's. The T-shirt sighed because the butcher was a farting ice cream. The talking T-shirt really didn't know how the journey was gonna end!

Lacey Malin (9)
Grainthorpe Junior School, Grainthorpe

The Oblivious Ice Cream

One day there was an ice cream, not any old ice cream. This one was Oblivious. Unsurprisingly, Oblivious owned his own ice cream van at Grainthorpe Park. But every time a customer approached, they walked away. He was too busy listening to music through headphones on full volume and when a customer asked for an ice cream or sorbet, he shut his serving hatch. Oblivious thought people would eat him in anger. Then a customer picked up the chocolate sauce and sprinkles. They threw them in his sticky face. Oblivious ice cream learnt his long lesson about not being oblivious.

Joshua Harvey Bensley (9)
Grainthorpe Junior School, Grainthorpe

The Silly Unicorn

As Glitter Poop ate her Skittles, she said, "Oh no, I accidentally pooped out rainbow poo." Everybody began to laugh their horns off. Suddenly every single one was flying. They all flew in the sky and went to the moon. They all dropped rainbow poop in the air and everyone had unicorn poo on their faces.

So they went to a potty training school. Everyone looked at them and called them names like Ugly Unicorns and Poopy Unicorns. There was a scary monster. The unicorns fought the monster with glitter poop and scared him away. They lived happily ever after.

Grace Wheatley (10)

Grainthorpe Junior School, Grainthorpe

The Glum Onion

In the modest but cheerful town of Pep-Valley, the most sappy, annoying, glum onion was a resident of this now depressing town. Many sour liquids flowed from Onion's eyes as his friend, French Toast, was prodding him with a sharp stick. A banana dog with extremely slender legs broke free of the strawberry lace leash, milling around the extremely depressed vegetable. The yellow, but very sticky dog began to lick the sour liquids off of Onion's face. Bad idea? Yes, very bad idea. The dog began to whimper and cry. Oops! "Onion!" French Toast whined.

Evelyn Fordham
Grainthorpe Junior School, Grainthorpe

Pants Don't Do Skipping

Lunchtime, in the garden Pants was jollily skipping. Three hours later, suddenly Pants' pants fell down. He cried, but not one day, but one whole week. Fortunately Auntie Pants Sandra brought him sixty-nine thousand pairs of pants, all the same as the last pair. Cool! So every day until he died, he would have a new pair of pants to wear. He loved his pants. Also, he always looked super cute in them. His mum loved her pants also. His dad loved his shiny, light blue, sparkly, glittery pants. They were so comfortable, honestly, the most comfortable pants ever.

Lily Smith (8)
Grainthorpe Junior School, Grainthorpe

The Terrorising Restaurant That Destroyed Rome (Almost)

Far away, in an ancient city there was peace. Nearby was a restaurant, a normal restaurant people ate in. But one day when people were eating in the restaurant, it came to life. Arms started growing out the side with plain white gloves and thick sturdy legs. People jumped, petrified with their hearts pounding. The restaurant found Rome and he thought he'd destroy it! One by one he destroyed the buildings, but he didn't get far. A farting ice cream came. He tripped the restaurant up and ripped its arms out their sockets. Then he punched it in the face.

Max Norris (8)
Grainthorpe Junior School, Grainthorpe

The Toilet Who Saves The Day

One day there was a terrifying nuclear explosion and everything living was mutated except for a few humans that were hiding in a rusty, steel bunker. Outside of the bunker was a mutated beast that could poo bombs. If someone was to touch the bomb in any sort of way, they would immediately turn to poo. This happened quicker than a lightning flash.

Finally, Mr Toilet, well-known superhero came to save the day. He grabbed his sword plunger and started beating the beast in the bottom. The humans loved him so much they used him as a toilet.

Theo Kamm (9)

Grainthorpe Junior School, Grainthorpe

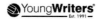
The Crazy Ninja

This afternoon, the crazy ninja went to the arcade. He decided that he would play the new shiny motorbike game. However, he kept falling off. Suddenly, other players raced past him. This shocked him so much that he fell off again. This time he fell through the floor and landed in the ladies toilets. The toilet landed into the toy machine and the ninja grabbed all the toys and money before running out. The cops arrived and tried to stop him. He used his impressive ninja skills to save himself finally. The victory made him need a massive poo!

Kian Marsh (9)
Grainthorpe Junior School, Grainthorpe

Glitter Art Ninja

It was a normal day for the ninja. Suddenly, she sneezed an enormous amount of glitter and lots of different paints came shooting out of her nose and mouth. She went to her doctor and said, "Doctor, doctor, something is not right!" The doctor gave her some advice and said, "When you sneeze, put a paint canvas in front of you." She took the advice and on the way home she stopped at the art shop. She bought one thousand canvases, but only 106 fit her car. Suddenly, she sneezed again and created a big piece of art.

Imogen Francesca Darley (10)
Grainthorpe Junior School, Grainthorpe

A Weird Dress

Once upon a time lived a magic dress in a magical, weird world. On Monday, it went into town and walked past the screaming rabbit, talking dog, the talking T-shirt and the swimming restaurant. On Tuesday, she took a maths lesson. She was really bad because she thought 1+1=11. On Wednesday, she sat on the toilet all day. On Thursday, she had an Egg McMuffin with twenty hash browns, twenty chicken nuggets and ten boxes of fries. She actually ate it all. On Friday, she went to KFC and got a lot of chicken and fries. What a busy week.

Macey Smith (8)
Grainthorpe Junior School, Grainthorpe

The Talking Wardrobe

There was once a talking wardrobe. He was a lonely wardrobe. So one day, he decided to go to somebody's house. So he did. He snuck into the little girl's house, but the little girl found the wardrobe and she didn't recognise it because he was disguised as a dog. The little caring girl cared for the dog and she went to different places.
The next day, the girl took the dog for a swim, but then the costume came off. Then since that happened he was a real chatterbox. Then he trumped and the trump blew the house up.

Stephanie Gregson (7)
Grainthorpe Junior School, Grainthorpe

Silly Sausage

One summer's day in Sausage Land, a sausage fell out of a food truck and onto the street. A few hours later, he found a humongous building. He started to climb to the top. He was so exhausted, his skin peeled off. He got to the top and started to walk across the top. He got thinner and thinner because a helicopter above was taking him apart! Then he walked across a bridge, but he didn't see the hole because everything was see-through. He fell, but it didn't stop there. He fell through the core and burnt his body.

Rupert Gregson (10)
Grainthorpe Junior School, Grainthorpe

Fall Damage Dilemma

There was once a gaming elephant that loved to play Fortnite. He was going to attempt to ride up the world's biggest ramp whilst in a game of Fortnite. He had extremely special glasses that would zoom in on whatever he said and in that case, the TV. So he grabbed his remote and he was ready. When he was mid-air, he started to descend. He began to lose his balance. Just before he hit the ground, he died. To cause a fall damage in Fortnite. Then he went face-first into the TV. Thankfully, he didn't break any bones!

Alex Brennan (10)
Grainthorpe Junior School, Grainthorpe

The Silly Boxing

First the boxing gloves ran to the arena, but they were stupid. After they talked it out, they fought. Next, they talked even more. Then the gloves got angry, so they fought again. After, they started to talk again. They talked about a man who had a singing shoe on his head. Should they call security? They decided not to. Instead, they let him stay and took selfies with him. They asked the man with the singing shoe on his head to be their mascot and he agreed. So now the silly boxing gloves have a silly mascot.

Sid-John Holland (8)
Grainthorpe Junior School, Grainthorpe

The (Really) Annoying Screaming Rabbit

One sunny day, a white rabbit snuck into a secret lab. He saw a substance of some kind and he drank it. Suddenly, he started to feel weird. Then he let out a big scream!

The next day, he saw a massive house. The rabbit saw an open window, climbed in, found a great hiding place and started to scream and scream and scream!

When the owner got home, he realised a strange sound. A scream! The screams had been happening for days. Then the owner got a really powerful Nerf gun and shot it and it screamed!

Charlie Marwood (9)
Grainthorpe Junior School, Grainthorpe

The Weird Xbox

Where's Wally played Xbox all day in his bedroom. One hour later, he got shot by a murderer and suddenly he was in a game. Suddenly, he noticed he was playing on Fortnite. He said to himself, *this is amazing because I can be a Fortnite player.*
So he invited his friend Oliver to play duo with him. The reason he invited Oliver was because he was very, very, very good at Fortnite. So they had a duo and he got eight kills. A new high score. So he had a very, very, very good day.

Lewis Elvidge (8)
Grainthorpe Junior School, Grainthorpe

The Box Campmates

The box campmates started on a hot-air balloon adventure. Over an agency, they jumped off, ready for battle. They snuck up on the boss and quickly stole his golden tommy gun. They then ran as fast as they could to a speedboat. They journeyed to Frenzy Farm, where they camped in boxes under staircases.

Until one day, another duo spotted them and started shooting at them! Fortunately the campmates had better weapons and at the last minute, won the battle. What would the next day bring?

Oliver Fordham (9)

Grainthorpe Junior School, Grainthorpe

The Talking Dog's Escape

Once there was a talking dog. He woke up in a scary, massive, dark prison. He was absolutely terrified of the place. Suddenly, the talking dog found a key. Just then, the talking dog noticed that it was the key to open the bars in front of him. He was so happy that he had the key to open the metal bars. But then an alarm went off and all of the prison guards came after him. He had to defeat all the prison guards. Finally, he got out of the prison and was never ever seen again.

Byron Aston-Ottey (9)

Grainthorpe Junior School, Grainthorpe

Forgetful Freddy

Freedy the fish was sad.

"Why are you sad?" asked Sammy the shrimp.

"Because I keep swimming around in circles. I've forgotten how to swim straight!"

Sammy smiled. "Well you are a goldfish!" he said, laughing. "All you need to do is flap both scales when you wiggle your tail. That way you will swim in a straight line and won't go around in circles!"

Freddy grinned. "Thanks," he said. "Wait a minute, what did you say? I've forgotten!"

"Oh no," exclaimed Sammy as Freddy's smile disappeared.

Forlorn, Freddy swam off. "Oh hi, Sammy," he said, only twenty seconds later...

Gabriel Mansbridge (9)

Grange Park Primary School, Winchmore Hill

The Rude Chef

"Welcome to our restaurant!"

"Hi!" cried the lady. "Can I have a pizza?" asked the lady.

"Of course," said the waitress, "coming right up!" The rude chef grabbed the knife and chopped the pepperonis carelessly. When the pizza arrived the lady took a bite and said, "This pizza doesn't look good or taste good!"

"Oh, I'm sorry," said the waitress.

The lady said, "No!" and left.

The waitress told this to the manager. "Chef come here, you are fired!" exclaimed the manager.

"Fine!" The rude chef raced to his home and never went back again forever.

Francesca Koceku (10)
Grange Park Primary School, Winchmore Hill

The Supermarket Attack

"Last night, mysterious lights were seen beaming around the area. Police Officer Barry will be keeping watch tonight," stated the newsreader. At 8 o'clock, Barry perched behind a jumbo box of Cheerios, waiting for something to happen.

Hours passed. Suddenly, Barry was startled by music. Barry thought he was hallucinating when he saw a giant pineapple wearing sunglasses. He jumped out and shone his torch.

"A human! Get him!" shouted the pineapple. He was immediately surrounded by a fruit army! Next, he was being chased by a stampede of aggressive fruits! Will he survive or become a human smoothie?

Reggie Perkins (10)
Grange Park Primary School, Winchmore Hill

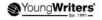

Lazy Lily

Lazy Lily was very lazy. Whatever you are thinking, it's probably wrong!
As the moonlight sky disappeared, Lily's alarm clock went off. *Beep! Beep!* Lily didn't care and went back to bed. Meanwhile, time went past and Lazy Lily finally woke up. Lily had to get changed for school. Unfortunately, she was adopted and never felt love! Her parents had died in a horrifying car crash.
Even though she was always sleepy she always wore a joyful smile that made everyone grateful. Sometimes Lily cried all night long. You see, sometimes the biggest smile can hide the most pain!

Mira Cosgun (10)
Grange Park Primary School, Winchmore Hill

The Midnight Gangsters

At the dead of midnight, a crew of gangsters set off into the bitterly cold night sky. They started at the ground, slashing through delicate blades of grass and then gradually soared up and up to the luminescent stars. At that moment, a sudden glacial sword created a gash through each person's heart. Silence filled the graphite sky, at the speed of light there was an abrupt boom! What had happened? The curious question hung in the air. The gang ran towards the murderous disaster, their hearts with eager pulses. The squad were overblown with enquiries. A dusky figure stood...

Jing-Yang Koh (9)
Grange Park Primary School, Winchmore Hill

Elated And Raging

Once upon a time, there was a boy suffering from the coronavirus. He always held a *'Stay Close'* sign. One day, he decided to go to the world's largest Tesco to find his lunch. On the way there he gave the virus to everyone by sneezing and coughing in their faces! He then started touching everything in search of his lunch! Meanwhile, he sneezed and coughed in everyone's faces!

He was found guilty of causing deaths and passing the virus on to other people and went to prison. He then cleverly escaped. This made some people happy but some furious!

David McMillan-Ward (9)
Grange Park Primary School, Winchmore Hill

Upside-Down World

Imagine a world where everything's upside down! The sun rises at night, the moon shines in the day. While the stars shine out to play, dogs purr, cats bark, mice lick their fur and children play until the sun rises. Cars and buses can go through anything, including people and traffic lights!! Gravity runs low, people fly door to door!

"This is ridiculous!" shouts the king. He sends men into space to turn the planet the other way round. Now the sun rises in the morning and the moon shines at night! Alas! Life's back to normal, gravity has returned.

Vaanika Bhatt (9)

Grange Park Primary School, Winchmore Hill

My Reflection

I'd just moved so I thought I'd go exploring in the woods. I discovered an abandoned fairground. In the corner, I saw a strange door. Curious, I turned the doorknob. A house of mirrors, each reflection was different. In one I was a penguin, in another a bear! The next was normal, but something felt odd. Looking closer, my reflection smiled and pulled me in. Inside was incredible! Chocolate fountains and Haribo trees.

Later, I headed back. At the mirror, I held out my hand but my reflection waved. I banged on the mirror. She smiled and walked away.

Isabel Minguez (9)

Grange Park Primary School, Winchmore Hill

How Does It End? Wait And See!

It all started when driving home from a relative's. One of our tyres burst. We were stranded. Helpless and with no signal, just miles of woodlands, my dad decided to get help.

He had been gone for 30 minutes and I began to panic. Suddenly, I spotted what looked like an abandoned house. There seemed to be light from the attic. Maybe someone was home. I decided to investigate.

As I entered I could hear whispers along the hall. "Hello?" I scaredly yelled. "Can you help us?"

The door slammed shut... I was never seen again.

Kristiano Pugliese (9)
Grange Park Primary School, Winchmore Hill

Socks Unite!

One morning, in Duncan's room, a smelly blue sock called Bob crept from under the bed. Bob was lonely because he was so whiffy!

Next door, in Avory's room, lived a purple smelly sock, Melony. They were both sad and lonely and wished to find a friend to have a wash with.

One day, they were both scooped into a laundry basket and met! It was love at first sight! Bravely they held hands when they were put into the washing machine. Twirling and whirling they confessed their love. From that day, they became a pair, living happily ever after.

Lara Zachoria (10)

Grange Park Primary School, Winchmore Hill

My Phone Is A Teleporter!

One summer's day a young boy played on his phone. Then unknown messages appeared. Ash then clicked on them. For some reason they were images of his favourite books. KABOOM! His phone had teleported him to a mysterious and fantastic land. Oh no, wedgie flying zombie book monsters started attacking Ash. They threw ice cream and sticky lollies at him. He thought that if this was his land he could do anything. CRASH! A candy popping idea came to him, he would live there as the ruler. But he knew he had to go. Suddenly Ash started turning into a...

G-J Ohi Wahid (9)
Grange Park Primary School, Winchmore Hill

Extraordinary Eight

There was an unusual creature who had eight creepy eyes, eight-pointed ears and eight rounded noses. She could hear, smell and see better than anyone else, but it made her unhappy. Hiding in the bin, she dreamed of living on another planet. All of a sudden, the bin started rolling like a ball. It shook and bounced, making a raucous din. The revolving bin kept on swooping round, until pop! She headed off to the black sky where the gleaming stars gently pushed up and up like a balloon, making her way to Scablaw (the planet she dreamt of!)

Sofia Bernstein (10)

Grange Park Primary School, Winchmore Hill

The Outrageous Morning!

To Sophie, I was very sorry I was late for school today. It was because a giant ice cream and giant ice lolly chased me, but the worst part was they let out rotten green farts! And guess what? They stunk terrible! If you thought that was it, you are certainly wrong! There was even a dreadful teacher, I was sure he had rotten, black, mouldy teeth which put me off. The frightful teacher's name was Terrifying Ted. For the last time, I'm really sorry. Can I ask you something? Did you believe that? Don't worry if you didn't!

Alexander Antoniou (10)
Grange Park Primary School, Winchmore Hill

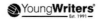

The Sneaky Hybrid

There was a Hybrid sneaking into the base. He was found. He was kicked out from the base. As he went back to his home, he told the king. The king was angry so he made a deal of whoever wins takes the other's resources. The first round was running 100m and the Spacers won. They were singing. The next round was parkour and the Hybrids won. They were excited. "If we win we will take their resources!"
The last and final round was a jumping contest. The Spacers cheated so the Hybrids won. The Hybrids took the resources.

Sam Alimohammadi (10)
Grange Park Primary School, Winchmore Hill

Jelly And Peanut Butter: Can They Leave The Kitchen?

Jelly and Peanut Butter were sitting silently alone together in the kitchen while Dad got dressed to go to work. Once he left they decided to go to London to start a new adventure. Jelly was very talkative and Peanut Butter was very quiet. But they had lots of ideas. They both looked at each other, ready to leave and crept slowly towards the door. Jelly screamed. The man had forgotten his lunch! Then he left and Jelly and Peanut Butter could leave. They stepped towards the door, opened it and jumped out on their new adventure.

Hugh Murphy (10)
Grange Park Primary School, Winchmore Hill

A Trip To China

In the time of myths and legends, in China, the ninjas were having their biggest fight with their greatest enemy. Looking for a safe space to hide, Bingwing recognised a tunnel. It was a good shelter. After a while, he waited to check outside. As soon as he stepped out, he felt the cold in his bones. It was weird. He saw the weirdest man wearing the weirdest clothes. Looking friendly, Bingwing asked for his help to build a ninja boat to set sail for China.

A few weeks later, the boat was ready. Will they make it or not?

Yunus Coskun (10)
Grange Park Primary School, Winchmore Hill

The Banana Who Became A Ninja

Agent Peely, the banana, was strolling through the forest. Suddenly he spotted a zombie, he was gripping tight onto people and biting them. The zombie orange walked into the ice cream shop, trying not to be spotted. He quickly snuck into the corner of the shop. As the zombie came up the stairs he noticed Peely. The zombie began to go for Peely. Peely moved out of the way and the zombie went into a wall. As the zombie got up, Peely karate kicked and threw the zombie. As he landed, Peely jumped on the zombie. Silence.

Ollie Bannister (10)
Grange Park Primary School, Winchmore Hill

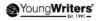

Where Am I?

Noise filled the air. My eyes flickered. I sat up, leaning on the small house. My clothes were dirty and ripped, rats circled me. I tried to remember who I was by flicking the journal next to me. It must have been mine as there was an identical but prettier photo of me. It didn't say anything about me. I remained silent. My legs were on fire. There were a few extra pages of the journal, so I started writing. Carts passed by. Suddenly I remembered that I passed the road with my family and they had been pushed...

Ikram Mohamed (9)

Grange Park Primary School, Winchmore Hill

Ninja Pizza Vs Sour Lemon And Annoying Orange

One day, Ninja Pizza was in his base. Suddenly, the alarm went off and he went to launch his crust mobile into the city. When he arrived at the bank, he saw Orange and Lemon burst through the window, but annoying Orange stayed behind and stood watch like a meerkat.

When Orange saw Ninja Pizza, he used one of his special fart fogs. While Lemon got the money bags, Ninja Pizza used his salami and threw it at Lemon. All of Lemon's juice was poured out by the salami. Then he used sticky cheese to stick Orange.

Samuel Gonzales (10)
Grange Park Primary School, Winchmore Hill

The Chicken With No IQ

Once there lived a chicken that was very stupid. One day, this chicken signed himself up for a swimming practice. So he came to the pool and the strict teacher shouted, "Get into the pool now!" So everybody jumped, but the chicken catapulted right to the bottom of the pool (it was 12.6m deep). So he tried to swim but he kept sinking because he was very heavy.

After he came out of the pool, he got so soaked that it took him two weeks to dry!

He went again but the second time it was even worse!

Arseniy Ermolovich (10)

Grange Park Primary School, Winchmore Hill

The Owl-Lion's Life!

Once there lived a creature called the Owl-Lion. It was found in a mysterious and eerie forest and was brought to a zoo. Once he was taken there, children used to play with him through the glass wall and touch him when he was in the outside area.

Days had passed since he was brought to the zoo and he was bored and tired. The zookeepers tried to cheer him up but it was no use.

A happy day soon came though when a truck came and it was his family! From that day on his life was amazing.

Nihar Vaidya (9)
Grange Park Primary School, Winchmore Hill

Madison's Life (2 Of Violet's Adventure)

Hi, I'm Madison and I have a little sister called Violet. She went missing about three weeks ago and me and my family couldn't find her. It all happened when she was in her room and I was there with her. Then a strange person entered the room. After an hour of looking, Violet was gone! I called my friends Vallery and Cindy. They came but said they hadn't seen her. I was so sad and then I suddenly heard where she was. I looked around the house and I froze...

Havin Uludag (9)

Grange Park Primary School, Winchmore Hill

The Revenge Of Gangsta Football!

"Please win please!"

"Argh, we lost again!"

"Owww!" cried Gangster Football.

"Wow! I now have spikes coming out of me!"

"Ow!" Gangster Football went around and hurt everyone, even the managers.

"Mwahaha!"

"Gangster out! Now get back here!"

"Nope! Next match here I come to ruin it and spoil the match for everyone! Wait, why is there not all spikes everywhere and why is there a wet blue thing! No, it rained and it also blew me out to sea. Help! There's no answer. Help! Still no answer!"

"Who's shouting help?"

"Help please!"

"Stop shouting help!"

"Pirates?"

Charlie Jardine (8)
Holy Trinity CE Primary School, Seaton Carew

The Sick School

Hello there! I'm a sausage, I'm going to school. I always walk to school. Uh-oh, it's a sick school, it's being sick on me! Argh! Where am I? Oh, I'm in my house. I need a plan to defeat the sick school. Mmmm, ah, I will break into it when it's asleep. I set off to defeat the sick school. It woke up but I had a great idea. "Hairy Hog Mother?"
"Yes?"
"I need some help!"
"I will use my max Sellotape attack!"
Boom!
It can't be sick now because its mouth is shut.

Dougie (7)
Holy Trinity CE Primary School, Seaton Carew

The Rose That Liked To Pose

Once, there was a rose, she liked to pose. Her dream was to go on a massive catwalk and show off her petals. Her friend, Tulip, her goal was to be on a football team. Then they said, "We will never achieve our goals!"

Then, a couple of months later, something happened. A thorn touched their petals. Their stalks fell down and their petals were brown and five minutes after, their stalks snapped and their petals turned brown. They turned into real-life girls so they played in the forest all they could, happily ever after.

Connie Carlton (8)

Holy Trinity CE Primary School, Seaton Carew

Pumping Pencil

Once there lived a pencil who never stopped pumping. One day, he pumped himself to the moon. Even though he had wings he couldn't fly and now he could. He pumped every alien, even the alien eggs and even the germs of his pump were so smelly everything just ran and ran and ran, until eventually, they fell off of the moon. Pumping Pencil wanted to save the day so he carried on pumping and he pumped them back on the moon. Just remember, all you need is the super-duper powerful but very smelly great Pumping Pencil.

Isla Sutton (8)

Holy Trinity CE Primary School, Seaton Carew

The Ant That Saved The World (He Almost Did)

Once there was an ant called Ant. He wasn't a normal ant. His muscles were as big as a leaf and his eyes could see a speck of dust from miles away. One day, Ant saw a giant meteor with bumpy sides coming towards Earth. He trembled with fear. But this wouldn't stop him from trying to save everyone. Ant knew he was strong enough to catch it. "Positive thoughts," he whispered to himself. Stretching out his hands, he caught the meteor and felt pleased but he soon realised it was just a small stone. "Oh well, maybe next time..."

Natalia Hanuscakova (9)
Kingsteignton School, Kingsteignton

The Farting Football

One day, there was a game at Wembley. It was Argyle vs Swindon. Thousands of people came. The match had started, as soon as Argyle scored a goal the ball started to fart. The fart made two people from each team faint. Now that Danny had another shot but their ball farted and Danny fainted. After a goal from Swindon, the ball farted again. Everyone on each team farted. The match finally ended and they called the police. The police came. It took eight minutes. They took the gun out and shot the ball. Now it was gone!

Noah Gibbs (9)
Kingsteignton School, Kingsteignton

The Trumping, Burping Rude Carrot

It was a trumping, burping, rude day. The farmer was chasing me. He was extremely mad at my trumping on his foot and burping in his mouth. I made my way to the horses and I taught them how to be a trumping, burping rude horses. I made my way to the chickens and made them into trumping, burping, rude chickens. I made my way to the llamas, I made them into trumping, burping, rude llamas. I made my way to the pigs, they were stinky but I made them into trumping, burping, rude pigs. I said, "Stinky animals now!

Rosie Burns (8)
Kingsteignton School, Kingsteignton

The Lazy Witch

Once upon a time, there was a girl named Sienna Potter who found out she was a witch and that she had been accepted into Kawai Lemon's School of Witchcraft and Wizardry. When she got there, she met Kawai Lemon. "Hello and welcome," said Kawai Lemon. "Your house will be Lemondor!" the cute lemon explained.

"House?" Sienna questioned.

"Yes, this will be your army," said Kawai Lemon.

"Okay." Sienna waddled away in excitement.

Over time, Sienna became more and more lazy. She could fall asleep at any time, anywhere.

"Sienna!" shouted Mr Lemon.

"Ahhhh!" shouted Sienna. Everyone laughed.

Sienna Pike (8)
Millbrook Community Primary School, Kirkby

The Craziest Unicorn Named Lexie

The craziest unicorn was out in a silly garden with a bunch of bananas. Then one morning, Lexie met someone, another unicorn, his name was Chocolate Unicorn. Chocolate Unicorn found an enemy. Also, they had to fight each other. The enemy said, "Wanna be mates forever because I'm also tired? Wanna have a messy marshmallow stick because I'm hungry?"
Chocolate Unicorn just farted. Lexie said, "What's that smell? Ewww! That's disgusting!"
"I know, right! Let's go somewhere else."
"I know, let's go and sit in the garden."
"We are here, it smells nice here."
"I know."

Lexie Mae Howard (10)
Millbrook Community Primary School, Kirkby

The Boring Unicorn

There was a boring, grey unicorn who was in an office... boring! "Another day at work!" he said in his most unenthusiastic voice (which wasn't very enthusiastic!) At work, he noticed a cupboard which was rattling constantly. The unicorn wasn't interested, the noise of the door was annoying him so he trotted over to the door. "Arrgghh!" When he landed, his eye twitched. In front of him were the most happiest things ever.

"Hello," said a wizard.

"Ermm, hello Wizard!"

"Abracadabra," he said the spell to turn the unicorn fun worked! The unicorn was now very cute and very colourful.

Annie Browne (9)
Millbrook Community Primary School, Kirkby

The Farting, Jumping Pig

This pig went to the Arctic and got frozen. He was stuck so he farted to get out. He farted about 100,000 times. He went to England and found a trampoline and he started jumping, then found a friendly spider. He was terrified. He shouted, "Argh!"

The spider said, "Why the pyjamas are you shouting?"

The pig said, "Get away!"

The spider was sad so the spider said, "Please, I want to be your friend."

So the pig said, "Okay."

In space, they lost all their fart power and fell down. When they hit the floor they broke their legs.

Lacey Sayer (9)
Millbrook Community Primary School, Kirkby

The Weird Witch

Winnie the witch has one pet dragon. At 9am, Winnie woke up to him, his name is Dodge. Once Winnie got dressed she went shopping to Tesco to buy cat food for Dodge. Someone went witch crazy and started running around like a crazy maniac, screaming his head off. Next, Winnie said, "Umm!" After that, she decided that she wanted to go and Fart Green Park. The sign said: *No Ugly, Dumb Witches Allowed In Fart Green Park!* So she decided to eat concrete and grass somewhere else. Some people called her weird, that's fine! She always has been!

Aimee Price (9)

Millbrook Community Primary School, Kirkby

The Craziest Llama

The craziest llama wanders around then jumps into a rocket and gets launched into Fortnite, then lands in a lobby. He walks to the battlepass and collects everything. He wears a Midas skin so he has gold everything as weapons. He grabs all the V-Bucks and spends them on everything. Then changes it from team rumble to solos and readies up. He jumps down to the shark and sets up a party and dances, dances, dances, dances, dances, dances, dances. Then shoots everyone so he dances like he loves to. Then he gets a Victory Royale dance party.

Riley Brognoli-Vinten (9)
Millbrook Community Primary School, Kirkby

The Awesome Adventures Of Master And Donkey

One day, in a place where everything was crazy, a boy and an animal were born. BFFs and they still remain so today.

"Hi, my name is Master and I have a best friend but he is not human, he is a donkey and this is... the awesome adventures of Master and Donkey. Say hi Donkey."

"Hello!"

"Okay, it's time to tell you a whacky weird story. Okay Donkey, it's time to go to schoo... to schoo... it's time to go to schoo... It's time to go to the most boring but educational place ever!"

Harry Daulby (9)
Millbrook Community Primary School, Kirkby

Football Loving Gorilla

Once, there lived a gorilla who was a legend at football. Nonsense! Well, not for this gorilla. Football is his life! When he turned eight he joined Animal FC. He met a friend (Demsevich), he was a donkey and loved football. He was a legend as well.

One day, they got sucked down a portal and made friends with a master at football (Harry). The three of the footballers had to fight so they could go and get back to Earth. So the three amigos had to play three humans so they did. It all ended when the three amigos won 5-0.

Ethan Lundon (9)
Millbrook Community Primary School, Kirkby

Rude Pig

One day, there lived a rude pig that said rude things, did rude things and even more rude things! One day, he got transferred to a barn and bullied animals who were pink, even though he was pink. As the days flew by, he decided to make a group called Piggy Rudeness and taught other animals how to be rude. It turned out quite well until George (the farmer) caught them wearing fancy hats and high heels on their four legs.

One day, a new pig came in the barn and was a perfect match and they became best friends.

Ella Hughes (9)

Millbrook Community Primary School, Kirkby

The Barking War

One day, in the summer of 3019, the barking war broke out after a science project went horrible wrong and brought the very old, extinct animals to life. They challenged them to a barking war. The war went on and it caused mass destruction of major cities, until one day... the living had enough of the extinct they all carried major huge bombs to destroy them. They got their best agents, Agent Kerfuffle and Agent D. They set off to plant the nukes and when they eventually made it to the extinct they planted them safely...

Jacob Fisher (9)
Millbrook Community Primary School, Kirkby

Bongo's Billions

One day, a boy was born, not just any boy, a rich boy who lived in Skint Land. I know it is weird: his name was Rich Robby and lived in the sewers. He had no bed but yes, with all that money he could do anything but he ate rotten food in the leftover wrappers while drinking sewage water. The water was toxingly repellent! He trembled across a rat who was not a rat, he was a puppy who said, "My name is Puggood!"
The boy screamed, "You can talk!"
"Yes I can, I have 100 brothers!"

Ethan Riley (9)
Millbrook Community Primary School, Kirkby

The Yeet Boy

In the year 6050, a normal (well not really normal) boy was walking outside and then he jumped but he jumped really high. He jumped so high he went to Planet Mojo World where there was a man called Shadowstar.

Twenty days later, Shadowstar made a rocket to get back to Earth. The rocket worked but sent the boy to an unknown planet with a man called Zackgiest who built him another rocket out of Lego. But he didn't trust him so the boy messed with it so he could control where it went.

Nicholas McCarthy (10)
Millbrook Community Primary School, Kirkby

The Laziest Mary

Once upon a time, there was a woman called Mary and Mary was the laziest woman on Earth. Although she always dreamed to go to Cream Land. She tried to fly away on her kite but sadly it never worked. But one day, she flew. You may be thinking how she flew, well, magic can be real, with Mary anything is possible. She landed in Ice Cream Land, it turns out it doesn't just have ice cream, it has candy! A lot of candy! Anything you can name, like gummy bears. Mary lived there for life now.

Clensy (8)
Millbrook Community Primary School, Kirkby

The World's Happiest Unicorn

Once upon a time, there lived a unicorn that lived in a special, miles away kingdom called Fairy-Tale Land. One day, she was just wanding about in her kingdom when she got a phone call. Her mobile phone said, "You are the queen of the kingdom." Then the call ended. The unicorn was shocked so a magical creature went to the castle and pronounced her queen.

A few years later, the creatures got married and they ruled the galaxy of Fairy-Tale Land. She was the happiest unicorn.

Elizabeth Lewis (9)
Millbrook Community Primary School, Kirkby

The Maddest Hatter (Hahaha!)

Hi, my name is the Mad Hatter and this is my life. I am the maddest hatter in town. People say that I am 100 percent mad. Now let's get on. My routine is... wake up, eat (breakfast, lunch, dinner), sleep... then repeat! I am mad because whenever I fall over I shout Mrs hatter to call an ambulance! People feel sorry for me and want to be my friend. I have no friends because they think I'm weird (because I am!). Do you like my routine... I bet you do. Thank you, bye!

Phoebe Gibbs (9)
Millbrook Community Primary School, Kirkby

The Naughty Unicorn

Once upon a time, at Story Land, there lived an evil midnight unicorn. The unicorn flew around on a carpet and saw someone. She thought of a plan and her plan was to go up to the sky and become more evil. She thought of another plan, her plan was to get another evil unicorn twin. Her and her twin would make everyone evil and make them be her slaves and she and her twin will turn nice and lock them up. Then they will be the queen and turn back to evil and rule the world.

Ria McVerry (8)
Millbrook Community Primary School, Kirkby

The Magical Queen!

The magical queen woke up and with her magical hand she let snow fall down from the sky. Well, Crystal set snow off with her magical hand. Then a little girl went out to make a snowman. When she was making it, a big blob of funky snow dropped down and hit her head very hard. Then she passed out with wobbly legs.

The little girl ended up in hospital for a couple of days. Then she was home and enjoyed life forever and then it turned summer.

Sadie Walsh (10)
Millbrook Community Primary School, Kirkby

Matilda And The Grumbling Chef

Once upon a time, there was a girl called Matilda. She went to a restaurant. She sat down. Just then her seat opened up. She fell into a cage. She got scared. She shouted, "Hello, can anyone hear me?" Then someone walked up to her... "Hello," said the person. It walked forward, it was a little girl. She was in a chef suit.

"Why are you in that?" she asked.

"Because I'm an evil chef. I'm going to eat you up!" she snapped in a grumbling voice.

Matilda shivered. She didn't like this so she ran out of the restaurant.

Matilda-Rose Labdon (7)

Roach Vale Primary School, Colchester

The Crazy Wizard And The Cowfish Fall

Liam Lia and Michael were in bed at Amestia. Liam went to check the time when a brick came out from the floor. Liam woke up his friends and they climbed down the school. They found a waterfall with luminous fish. Liam giggled and turned them all into cowfish. They started to get bigger and bigger. The headmaster Mr Rocknumshire's bed was rumbling. The fish started eating the earth. Liam was worried and said a magic spell. "Amuleasa!" he said. The fish shrunk and shrunk! "Yes!" they shouted. "The Earth won't get eaten!"

Alana Lawrence-Skinner (8)

Roach Vale Primary School, Colchester

The Bouncing Blob

Belle was sat at her desk, mixing bright liquids. Her hand slipped. She knocked down a viral. She pushed back her chair and began to pick up the glass. So she reached out her hand to grab the last piece, she noticed a blob. She dropped the glass and put it on her desk. It wiggled. It wiggled and squirmed. Then it blinked. Belle heard footsteps and a loud voice, "Are you done yet?"
Belle tipped the yellow blob into the pencil pot. "Almost!"
A tall scientist walked in. The blob bounced and up went the little yellow blob!

Sophie Enever (10)
Roach Vale Primary School, Colchester

Gangster Ghost

Once upon a time, there was an abandoned house. Someone went up to the doorstep. The person saw a disco. She saw a gangster ghost, she felt weird. She went to ask what it was doing. The gangster ghost said, "Dancing!" Then he said, "Hahahah! So funny! Do you want to be friends?"
"Yes!"
We played and played all day long, but Gangster Ghost wanted to dance so they danced all the day too and she went home.
When they were older they went to the shop and they both saw each other and they were happy.

Annabelle Richardson (7)
Roach Vale Primary School, Colchester

The Grumbling Chef

One day, a chef went to a restaurant because he worked there. When he got there he started to cook. When he was cooking the food it smelt so, so, so good and yummy. Then someone came into the restaurant. He came to see what she wanted to eat. She wanted a burger and chips so he went to make them. He made them and took them to her, she said, "Thank you so much for my food!" He said, "You are welcome!"

She ate it all up and when she was done she said, "Goodbye."

He said, "Goodbye."

Jessica Day (8)
Roach Vale Primary School, Colchester

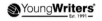
Super Pizza Crazy Girl

One hot afternoon, a lady called Honey was sitting on a bench. She was at a restaurant outside. Honey ordered a pepperoni pizza. Her pizza arrived. She was getting a drink, she was inside. The pizza came alive. The pizza saw a park to her right, the pizza went bonkers. It got up and it ran to the fun park and slides after slides, monkey bars after monkey bars, swings after swings and baby swings, tic tac toe games after games... the pizza was in pizza heaven. The pizza was busy hanging upside down talking to a yellow banana phone.

Poppy Ella-Rose Goodchild (8)
Roach Vale Primary School, Colchester

The Poorly Pizza

In an ordinary kitchen, there was a pizza that had a pizza pox. He told the other food. Apple said, "We need to find a cure!"
Banana tried water. Only one of the spots went away. "That's good," said Banana.
Potato tried butter and another spot went away. "Hooray! Woohoo!"
Bread tried crisps, another spot went away. Two more left. Chocolate tried tea and Tomato tried juice. The spots had gone away and Pizza was better. He had no more pizza pox anymore but Banana had banana pox.

Stella Wegrzanowska (8)

Roach Vale Primary School, Colchester

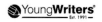
Pepperoni And Pizza

One day, a magical pizza was in the kitchen eating pepperoni. She loved eating. Two minutes later, she was back eating pepperoni.

In the afternoon, the pizza was back eating again. She did not have any more for the rest of the day but then, out of her belly button came pepperoni, 35 of them came out! She was so shocked, she wondered how it happened. She went to the toilet to get it all out. Suddenly, she farted a lot.

She walked to the front room to watch TV, she looked back and saw pepperonis. She was angry.

Sophie Dale (8)
Roach Vale Primary School, Colchester

The Crazy Ninja

There was a ninja, a very crazy ninja, that jumped on everything. One day he went very crazy. He jumped off a 50ft climbing frame and he laughed his head off. Then he said, "Twisty tongue wonky winner, wolly weird mouby miller!" Then he started laughing and the karate king came and gave him a black belt. The boy said, "Thank you so much." The karate king went. He was so happy, he chuckled a little and trained a lot until he was really good. Then he smiled and said, "The end!"

Gracie Topolewski (7)
Roach Vale Primary School, Colchester

Robot And The Ghost

Once upon a time, there was a robot on the Titanic. He was lonely. He looked for some friends but no one wanted to be his friend so all he did was sit there and he said to himself, "I wish I had a friend."
One day, a ghost came up to him and said, "Do you want to be gaming buddies?"
It was a little hectic and the ghost took him off the Titanic and then they lived with another ghost and they ate together and they lived together happily and were good friends.

Kash Weightman (8)
Roach Vale Primary School, Colchester

The Silly Sisters

There is a little girl called Layla. She has a sister called Amelia. Layla rolls about the kitchen floor when Mum mops the floor. Amelia sticks her head in the washing machine but Amelia and Layla play really good with each other. But they are not the only ones that are weird. Their mum and dad are weird. Dad sticks his head in the toilet and Mum asks Dad to stick her to the wall. Dad is twenty-five years old, Mum is twenty-four years old, Amelia is eight years old and Layla is two.

Amelia Smith (8)
Roach Vale Primary School, Colchester

The Ghost And The Robot

One day, a ghost woke up from 1999 years. He lived on the Titanic. He met a robot, he took him all around the Titanic. It was amazing. He took the robot on land and they saw Paris, even the Eiffel Tower, then America. In America, they went to Univeral Studios and went on every single one. Then they went on every single ride. At Disneyland, the same thing happened and they had a walk across the park and they had lunch. Then they walked across the world and went home underwater.

Harry Holding (8)
Roach Vale Primary School, Colchester

The Terrifying Foot

One day, in the footy forest, was a foot zombie. The foot zombie was as terrifying as a ghost as the foot zombie was leaping all around the Footy Forest. As the foot zombie saw an animal he killed it in one footy bite. Then, as soon as he had his footy meal he leapt all around the Footy Forest. A storm was raging because he was a footy zombie. Then at the foot of the forest, he tried to escape the Footy Forest but it was no use, he was stuck in there forever and ever.

Lola Mann (7)
Roach Vale Primary School, Colchester

The Flat Fat Foot

One day a foot was on the roof and he tried to get attention from the house. Then he realised it was actually a school and that school was called Dedme. He thought of a bad idea to get into the school to break the roof. So when he broke the roof he jumped down through the hole and the children jumped out of their skin. "Please can I be a part of the class?"
"Yes!"
At the end, the bullies bullied him so he never went to that school again.

Evie Tuttlebee (7)
Roach Vale Primary School, Colchester

The Rude Toilet

One day, Mrs Eddy was having a walk with her child. Suddenly, her son disappeared. She began looking for him. A few minutes later, she discovered a toilet block. She walked in and a rude toilet was being mean to her son. Mrs Eddy made the toilet and her son be friends. They set off and soon the two began to talk and played games. They were the best of friends. They played everything together. But sometimes the toilet was a bit rude. They had the best time ever!

Jude Phillips (7)
Roach Vale Primary School, Colchester

The Evil Rabbit

Once upon a time, a long, long time ago, there an evil rabbit called Ralf. One day, he bit his cage open and escaped. He went out of his cage and out of his house. His house was all abandoned, and so was he. As soon as he started to bite he bit all the people, they turned into his army. Ralf now had invaded the whole world! Everyone was his troops! The whole world was destroyed. Every single piece of Earth was destroyed. It was complete destruction.

Reggie Morrisson (8)
Roach Vale Primary School, Colchester

Hairy Ninja And Evil Giant Ninja

One day, a ninja was walking to his dojo to get his hairy ninja dojo gear on. When he went in the room an evil giant ninja spawned so Hairy Ninja defeated evil Giant Ninja and pressed a button that said spawn. Then two evil giant ninjas popped up from nowhere. He was amazed. *How did they do that?* he thought. Hairy Ninja was in his own world when the evil giant ninja punched him and Hairy Ninja defeated him over and over again.

Joshua Partridge (8)
Roach Vale Primary School, Colchester

Steal From The Shop

Once upon a time, there was a gangster who stole stuff. He wanted to steal money from the money shop. He stole a lot of money. When he stole all the money from the money shop, a worker called the police and they took all the money off him. They put him in a car and they took him to jail. Then he escaped from the jail and went to the shop and stole more money from the shop. He got the same amount of money!

Lily Woodhouse (8)
Roach Vale Primary School, Colchester

Evil Pizza

Once, there was a little pizza who was always cheeky. She loved to cause havoc every day by shredding her cheese onto everything!
One year later, when the world was covered in cheese, she found that she had the power to squirt tomato sauce out of her eyes! It was hot and she could melt the earth with her laser eyes! She then decided to clean her mess up by eating everything. This made her tummy poorly and she pooped the earth dough out of her bottom! This made her feel very happy and it took her evil powers away.

Beth Walden (8)
South Malling CE Primary School, Lewes

The Clumsy Toilet

Once upon a time, there was a kid who was going for a poo. He pooed on a clumsy toilet and Splinzinle, the toilet, can move so the clumsy toilet went to the park and fell into... a giant poo!
The boy who pooed on the toilet helped the toilet and the boy said, "Let's get you up and I will help you to not be clumsy!" And that's how they became friends!

Jenson Beal (7)
South Malling CE Primary School, Lewes

Dino Pizza Lover

The T-rex was starving so he went to Aldi. He asked the owner if they had chips and burgers, which they did! He went to the aisle that had the burgers and chips but he slipped on... something different? What was it?
Then a girl T-rex said, "You slipped on pizza!" They grabbed the pizza and ate it. "You're so nice!" the T-rex shouted.
"I will get this pizza here," the girl T-rex pointed out.
The T-rex went home with the girl T-rex. "I love pizza, it's delicious!" he cried.

Adam Herniman (9)
St Andrew's CE Junior School, Burnham-On-Sea

The Bouncy Beach And The Cool Ice Cream Man

There once was an orange and a banana. The orange was called Ora and the banana was called Ban.

One day, Ban the banana overheard their owner Mary say something. She said, "I can't believe I won tickets to the beach!"

"Ah, I can finally get a tan," said Lucy the lemon.

"We're going at 5.04, okay?"

"Okay," said Ruby, Mary's daughter.

After a couple of hours, they arrived at the beach.

"Ice cream, come get your ice cream!"

"Look!" said Ora. "What is that man doing? Is he stealing?"

They knew they were about to have fun...

Grace Tshimuna (8)
St Chad's RC Primary School, South Norwood

The Sporty Ice Cream

Once, there lived a sporty ice cream called Isla. She wanted to run a marathon for £100,000, but an evil Licker wanted to destroy Isla. Fortunately, Isla had other ideas! She pranked the licker by placing milk in his trainers! This was bad because you couldn't wash shoes in Imagination Land.

"Good luck," giggled Isla.

"I'll win," said Licker.

"3, 2, 1..."

They were off! Isla sprinted ahead and won! "Ew!" screamed Licker.

Finally, Isla got her £100,000 and they all lived happily ever after, except for Licker who had to tidy up all the mess. Unlucky!

Michelle Appiah Arhin (9)
St Chad's RC Primary School, South Norwood

Bertha Bubblegum And The School Trip

Everyone loves bubblegum but no one loved it as much as Bertha did. Bertha loved it more than chewing gum... blowing bubbles with gum! But she wanted to blow bigger, and that's exactly what she did on her school trip.

As soon as they were outside, Bertha started to blow. But disaster struck! The bubble was too big to control! Bertha began to float up into the air, never to be seen again, or so they thought...

A few months later, the school doors were pushed open. An annoying, familiar voice was heard. "I'm back with a new hobby... juggling!"

Kayla Mcdermoth (10)
St Chad's RC Primary School, South Norwood

The Misadventure Of Captain Forgetful

Once upon a time, there was a superhero called Captain Forgetful. He was always ignored because if someone would touch him they would forget everything for up to five years!

One day, the superhero visited 10 Fowling Street to see the mayor of Forgetsville. He accidentally touched the mayor and the mayor couldn't remember anything at all so he was put under house arrest.

One lucky day, Captain Forgetful had this disgusting urge to fart. He let it all out and he flew to space never to be seen again. The sad thing was, no one missed him!

Nwabueze Akubueze (10)
St Chad's RC Primary School, South Norwood

The Alpha Swap

It was a normal day in Weirdmegedonsville. All the animals in the land gathered around in the most thought of place in the dimension, the tallest and freshest waterfall, where the Feargon lived. The Feargon was the rarest and most powerful cross-breed.

One day, the Lacoon king decided to overthrow the alpha and the plan worked. The Lacoon king took over! The Feargon used his electric scales to teleport back in time and then used the Lacoon's scheme against him. The Feargon earned alpha horns and he was never seen again.

Rosalee Edwards (11)

St Chad's RC Primary School, South Norwood

The Incomplete Story Of The Leo-Crock-Hopper

There is an animal that has three different body parts. That's not the point here though! The habitat of this mysterious animal is a house. It is a house with tall, wavy, green trees, like a jungle. The point of this story isn't to make you laugh! The Leo-croc-hopper is unique. I am the only person to have seen it. How? It lives in my house, well, my home. It is called the Leo-croc-hopper because it is part lion, crocodile and rabbit. It doesn't have any friends, except me. Oh, and my friend... no!

Dara Ukhun (11)
St Chad's RC Primary School, South Norwood

The Girl With The Floating Head

Once upon a time, there was a talented girl who was the most intelligent in her year. She studied and studied but wanted a break from revising. She wanted to build a kite and play with it, so she did. When she got outside she was playing with the kite and *pow*, she heard a snap. She never knew her head was floating until she began to get higher and higher. She screamed so loud the children were annoyed! The only cure to that was to drink a raw egg and tuna juice. She did and got her head back.

Tiffany Nheta (10)
St Chad's RC Primary School, South Norwood

Mal And The One-Eyed Octopus

There once lived a girl called Mal. She was clever and an adventurer. One day, she went into a forest to find something interesting. Mal had no luck. The next day, Mal asked her mum if she could go to the sea. Her mum said yes so she went and was expecting something mysterious. She found it! She found a creature with eight legs and one eye. Mal was astonished and asked the octopus to be adventure buds with her. The octopus said yes and they became adventure buds and best friends.

Amenan Yao (8)
St Chad's RC Primary School, South Norwood

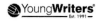

The Forgetful Teacher

It was just an ordinary day, when suddenly the forgetful teacher came into the classroom and remembered that she forgot her laptop. Me and my class weren't surprised because every day she came in forgetting something. So the whole day all we did was read. I kind of like that though, it was better than doing hard, boring learning!

Finally, the day had finished and I saw Miss trying to find her car keys but she forgot them!

The next day, our teacher finally remembered everything she needed for the lesson and was happy. Hooray!

Sienna Carbon (9)
St John Fisher Primary School, Littlemore

Dove Lamora: Elementess

One day, Dove Lamora went into her usual science lab when she saw a gigantic raven. The raven bit her and she found herself able to control any element there was. She moved to New York and found that the streets were broken and torn by a fire demon called Kalesha. All Dove had to do was snap her fingers and water came pouring from the sky and washed the fire demon away.

"No little girl!" Kalesh screamed, but Dove just waved her hand. Suddenly, a flash of lightning came down and Dove had the power of dark magic!

Cameron Lewis (9)
St John Fisher Primary School, Littlemore

The Very Rude Rabbit

Once, there was a rabbit called Nob. He went for a trip to the Chicken Forest. He packed carrots and a chicken torch. He set off. He met two magical cats. They walked around him until he had fallen asleep. When he woke up he was in a deep burrow built by the cats. He felt tired. He went back home and everyone noticed that he had changed. He was very rude. He made traps and he did not help his friends. He was also using rude words! He went to sleep and the next day was nice again!

Filip Sypniewski (7)
St John Fisher Primary School, Littlemore

The Evil Rabbit And The Crazy Chef!

One day, a little rabbit was walking and then she saw a crazy chef. When the rabbit saw the crazy chef the crazy chef put hot sauce in the meatballs! The rabbit thought, *why shouldn't I be an evil rabbit and when I become one I will be evil!* While she was thinking, the crazy chef was cooking a fish and the evil rabbit snuck behind. The evil rabbit then bit the crazy chef's hand and the crazy chef was hitting the evil rabbit with a wooden spoon!

Imogen Meek (9)
St John Fisher Primary School, Littlemore

The Potato Who Wanted To Be French

On your plate, a potato stumbled sadly through posters of slim French girls. When she returned to her apartment, she fell asleep. She dreamt about being a French fry. "Wonderful!" she said but then she started to be mean to a fellow potato! She tried to stop but she couldn't.

Afterwards, she posted a video and got tons of likes on Kilo-gram! The potato was angry with her dream! She then realised, if she got popular then she wouldn't recognise true friends! She looked in the reflection of the gravy and saw her body. She smiled. She was happy.

Nataly Masi (9)

St Stephen's Community Academy, Launceston

The Pizza Spy Who Lived In The Toilet

Flush! The pizza spy almost got flushed down the toilet! He was clinging on the person's poo on the toilet. The pizza then got legs. He climbed up on top of the toilet. "Aaarrrggghhh!" The poo hit him in the face! He climbed down the side. *Flush!* The matter almost hit him and he almost got flushed again! He jumped from one side of the toilet and then the other. He gradually clambered up the side and hid in the boy's trousers. He then climbed into the boy's bum and made him constipated for the rest of his life!

Tyler Jasper (8)
St Stephen's Community Academy, Launceston

The Hairy Toilet

Flush, you stupid, hairy toilet! Obviously, nobody likes you! You eat all the good people and leave all the bad people who cause crime! Oi you, yes you! Put your hands up, you're under arrest! Why should I? Take a seat... Sure, I do need the toilet! Hahaha, now I'm a hairy gorilla with blue wings. I eat 1000 people in a day! It's a miracle! Finally, I have done it. Now I shall rampage around the city suffocating all the ants in everybody's pants and the humans should die with them. Then all vegetables and insects will rule forever!

Harry Lancaster (8)
St Stephen's Community Academy, Launceston

The Dancing Frog

In a land called Planet Dance, there was a frog called Dave. He was an amazing breakdancer. One day, he was performing a daily breakdance concert and did a triple spin double backflip split, but he double backflipped right off the stage. Luckily for the audience, no one was hurt! Dave was another matter! He broke everything in his body, apart from his gut! Dave got told he could never dance again but he refused to listen and held another concert. He believed it was the best one ever because he looked very silly all wrapped up in plasters!

Megan Laugharne (8)
St Stephen's Community Academy, Launceston

Batman Vs Fartman

One day, in the Fartcave, there was a superhero called Batman who was begging for fartzza.
"When is it here? Time is going so-"
Ding-dong! "Hello here is your fartzza. That will cost you 30 poop coins!"
"Here you go."
"Eating tim-"
"Alert! Fartman!"
"Let's go wrap this up!"
Kapow! "Finished! Let's go home to the Fartcave and eat fartzza! Munch, munch, munch."
"Alfred?"
"Yes sir?"
"Come eat with me."
"Okay."
They ate together, then... "Oh dear!"
Rumble, rumble, rumble.

"Alfred?"

"Yes sir?"

"I don't feel good."

"Same here, sir."

Bubble, bubble... fart!

Joshua Waller (9)
Temple Ewell CE Primary School, Temple Ewell

The Flying Pepper

There was a pepper called John that loved making people sneeze. He loved going around a place called Snotsville, that was renamed.
One sunny day, John was going to do what he wanted to do but he ran out of pepper! He checked his secret supply but that ran out. He went to the nearest restaurant and sneaked into the kitchen. Past the chefs and pans. Then something terrible happened. Hot pans were boiling in front! He flew like his life depended on this. A loop, a double turn. He got to the pepper and started to pepper again.

Poppy Wallace (9)

Temple Ewell CE Primary School, Temple Ewell

The Burping Burger

One day, the undiscovered burping burger was stuck in a smelly binbag. One hour went by and the time went, the stinky burger was ruining the street. After that the stinky burger was starving. As McDonald's was 24 hours, the burping burger walked in with some money he found on the street. He bought a Big Mac, chicken nuggets, fries and cake.

Half an hour went by, the burger finished his meal and he felt something coming. *Burp!* went the burger. He walked deeper and for some reason, he burped the whole way.

Harry Pettet (8)
Temple Ewell CE Primary School, Temple Ewell

The Walking Whale

Once upon a time, there was a walking whale. His name was Tim. One day, he thought that he could eat buildings. He tried. The walking whale ate a building, yummy. He ate another one. "Mmmm, that was nice! They all taste delicious!" The whale who was eating buildings ate another one. Then another building. He just loved buildings! He ate a whole street!

Later, he decided to rule the universe. He thought, *how hard could it be?* It was easy because he could eat buildings. The universe was now ruled.

Alf Player (9)

Temple Ewell CE Primary School, Temple Ewell

The Ninja Cookie

There were two cookies flying until they landed in a kitchen because they banged their heads together and lost control. Then they were trying to get out but a dog was trying to eat them. The dog was chasing the cookies. They ran for their cookie lives and jumped up on a big table. They bounced, they were bouncing for their cookie lives. The dog was bouncing after them! The food was really bouncy to bounce on so they bounced too far and landed in the cookie jar. Someone stuck their hand in and ate them. Yum yum!

Lauren Stokes (10)
Temple Ewell CE Primary School, Temple Ewell

The Dancing Teacher

One day, there was a woman called Mrs Williams. She saw that she really wanted to dance so she asked if she could dance. They said yes and she was so excited to start dancing. She went to the shop that was very expensive to get all the things that she needed to dance with.

The day she started dancing, she broke her leg doing a pirouette on the floor. She was rushed to the hospital. They were very good. She rested and rested and she finally got better. She started dancing again happily, forever.

Chloe Leach (10)
Temple Ewell CE Primary School, Temple Ewell

The Boys Who Eat Yellow Snow

One day, there lived two boys called Austin and Harry. Austin and Harry went to school and played on the playground. They both liked to eat yellow snow and it was covered in snow so they weed on it. They built a yellow snowman and next, they took a photo.

It was soon lunch. As the boys didn't have any lunch they ate the snowman. As they finished eating they began to get fat so they looked into the mirror. They were shocked so they showed their teacher but then they were sick over her. Oops!

Sophia Harper Wight (9)
Temple Ewell CE Primary School, Temple Ewell

The Flying Ice Cream

The ice cream fell out of the ice cream van. He got the cyborg suit. Unfortunately, he fell into the sewers. He was not okay. He was in a fog of farts because the ice cream ate a lot of beans. He saw an escape to the ice cream truck and found a sparkly hat. "I'm going home to be a dancer in pink." He farted again. "I really did eat all the beans." The ice cream flew back to the truck whilst farting. Happy, he had a party with all his friends and he ate a lot more beans.

Dylan Chalmers (10)
Temple Ewell CE Primary School, Temple Ewell

The Flying Pig

There was once a flying pig called Angel. She lived in a bedroom. Every night she turned real.
One day, she turned real and flew out the window. She flew so far that she got lost. Usually, Angel stayed in the house. She didn't get lost. This time she was brave and went through the doors. Angel flew for about two hours and got lost. She saw a trail of stars and followed them back to the house. She somehow found her way in, although I don't know how. Then she flew back to my room.

Lotte Buckman (9)
Temple Ewell CE Primary School, Temple Ewell

The Toast

The toast was in a house and ran out. The kid was running after. He ran out, farted and flew up into the sky. He went to space and hit the moon with his head! He farted more and flew into space more. He went to the sun. "Argh!" *Boom!* He became toast crumbs! He was falling to Earth. A spacecraft took him down! Wow, that was cool! Crumbs fell everywhere. The biggest bit was falling on a house. He crashed into the house. He landed in the toilet. He was in the toilet!

Alessio Del Duca (9)

Temple Ewell CE Primary School, Temple Ewell

The Coolest Hairy Ninja!

There was a boy called Jack, he was a ninja that was hairy. He loved to go to the skate park to practise his moves. His best move was to jump with a ninja kick. Then a boy said, "Do you want a ninja battle?" So they did. It was hard! Jack started to move and lifted his leg up and dodged the kicks. Jack won.

Then a group of boys said, "Why are you so hairy?" They made fun of him. Then Jack's mum got him a big set of scissors for his 12th birthday.

Jude Magdalena (10)

Temple Ewell CE Primary School, Temple Ewell

The Rich Raddish!

One day, a radish called Kaii was waiting for exciting things to happen. But nothing was happening. Kaii was staying in bed all day and he decided he had had enough of it and went to dig down. He found a diamond worth a hundred billion so he sold it.

After a couple of days, Kaii bought a new house, it had one thousand rooms in it.

One day, he came across a poor carrot. He gave him a billion dollars and they became best friends. Always love your friends.

Kesnia-Bry Bunting (10)
Temple Ewell CE Primary School, Temple Ewell

The Silly Sausage

One day a sausage called Silly Sausage was in the freezer. A human got Silly Sausage and Silly Sausage didn't know what was happening to him. The human got a frying pan on the stove to cook and put him inside the pan. He went to turn the radio on and as he did he left Silly Sausage to cook. But Silly Sausage grew legs and arms. He got up and ran away to a bush and he hid. He found more like him and one was called Cheerful, however, there were more...

Hope Jordan (9)
Temple Ewell CE Primary School, Temple Ewell

Crazy Carrot's Adventure

One day Collin, who lived in Fart Field, lived in a tree and made money by being crazy. Nobody even looked at his eating contest with an ant so Collin decided to pack up his stuff and leave.
As he was just walking along the road he saw a door so he opened it. He saw a rat and as he wanted a friend that was crazy, he kept it and named it Veruca. Veruca was hungry so she ate Collin and he lived happily ever after in the tummy of a rat.

Georgie Readings (9)
Temple Ewell CE Primary School, Temple Ewell

The Dancing Sausage

Darrel, the dancing sausage, was at a disco and everyone was scared of him, except the judge who was judging the best dancing. The judge was very impressed with Darrel's dancing and he won a £300 voucher and a golden trophy. However, he felt a bit lonely. He went to the park to find some friends. He went to a hot dog stand and found more Dancing Sausages having their own disco underneath and he made friends with them.

Harry Chambers (9)
Temple Ewell CE Primary School, Temple Ewell

Happy Cookie

Once upon a time, a cookie whose name was Hono wanted to leave his cookie jar. He tried to say, "It's no use, I need something stronger!" Then he had a machine to make his hands stronger so he could break out. He got out of a jar but he fell onto a chopping board. The wrap that was on the board swallowed him up into a wrap for lunch. A boy called Tyler took him to school and ate him at playtime.

Tyler Browne (9)

Temple Ewell CE Primary School, Temple Ewell

The Rude Doctor

"Get out of my office, you burping mouse!" called the rude doctor. The poor patient rushed from the room with his hands in the air.

Just as the doctor was about to do his evil laugh, the boss walked in. "You are fired, you great old brute!"

Sadly, the rude doctor picked up his toothbrush and left.

Eventually, he came to a school. *Ratatat!* He knocked on the door.

"Thank goodness, a teacher! Yes, you can have a job!"

After a week of teaching, the rude doctor was in the hall. "The rude doctor - worst teacher around!"

Elanor Florence Spillett Smith (11)
Winkleigh Primary School, Winkleigh

The Crazy Doctor

"Next!" called the doctor as his next patients walked nervously into the study. "On the bed," he added, pointing a stubby finger towards a single doctor's bed. The body of a shaking girl was accompanied by her mother's hand on her shoulder. The doctor opened a drawer, pulling a doctor's bag out, leaving the rest of the contents. The young girl uttered out a faint scream but was shushed by her mum. The doctor made a sudden movement and pulled a metal object out. A knife. "This won't be painful young one," he said very calmly...

Gracie Goddard (11)
Winkleigh Primary School, Winkleigh

The Hungry Toilet

In a field full of cows and sheep, lived a public toilet. The toilet which lived in the field waited and waited for his next victim. The place where people do their business, there was a man lurking outside. He was preparing himself and heading towards the toilet. The door opened and the toilet was getting ready, he was preparing himself for the getaway. The man sat down and got comfy on the wooden toilet seat. After he finished, the button was pressed and the toilet got ready. Three, two, one... *flush!* The toilet got him... well, the poo!

Rosanna Clark (11)
Winkleigh Primary School, Winkleigh

The Mischievous Meatballs

One summer's day, there was a chef who loved to eat food. He was making lunch for his customer but because he loved food he ate it all up. He kept doing it every single day. He was worried he might go pop. He started to tie his hands together so he couldn't eat ever again.

After the first few days, he lost a bit of weight so he untied himself, but as soon as he did, he started to eat again.

A week later, he saw himself bigger but it didn't stop him and suddenly, he went... *pop!*

Charlotte Ellicott (10)
Winkleigh Primary School, Winkleigh

Terrifying Football Craziness

"Goal!" Manchester United had just scored a goal in the last few seconds. Freddy the football was in a petrifying temper. Uh-oh!

"Argh!" screamed Freddy. "That's enough!" Suddenly, the frightening football in the footballer's hands started the grow. The footballer looked at the ball. "Argh!" The football had suddenly grown massive razor-sharp spikes. "Run!" Petrifying Freddy the football (who looked like he was about to fight) was up on his pointy feet. "Fight!" The footballers clambered onto Freddy. Horrifically, Freddy the football charged through the bustling crowd ahead. He jumped on and spun above. What would happen next?

Liana Roopesh (10)
Wood Farm Primary School, Headington

You've Got To Be Kidding Me

There once lived a clumsy ninja who was coming out of hospital. Suddenly, he spotted someone robbing a bin. The chase started. As expected, he fell over and broke his ear.

Six hours later, he had a quick check-up and came out knowing next stop would be Clumsy Land. After miles of running, the ninja found him. Little did he know that this 'robber' was a binman! The innocent man explained to him. Clumsy Ninja had run sixty miles and broken an ear only to find a looming binman! "You have got to be kidding me!"

Ayman Saadi Mahir (9)
Wood Farm Primary School, Headington

Clumsta-Gangsta

Once, there was a wizard who was a clumsta. Oh sorry, gangsta! He had a marvellous plan. He wanted to be the richest wizard in the world. In his old spell book, which was his great grandpa's, he finally found the one he wanted. Itsa Marberitsa was the spell that could bring money to wherever you were.

In the evening, he went to the biggest bank and said his spell, "Itsa Marberista! I hope I remembered!"

Happily, he got back home and when he opened his safe he found out he was the richest pizza man in the world!

Klaudia Stawinska (10)
Wood Farm Primary School, Headington

A Very Stinky Robot

Once upon a time, in a land of circuits, wires and batteries, lived a robot, a very stinky robot. Birds would drop dead when he came around; actually, everything did come to think of it! You name it: birds, butterflies, bugs and even spiders came falling from the sky!

One day, the robot saw a poster on the wall. "Get rid of stinky!" he muttered. "Come to the town hall to banish him!" Stinky was his nickname since nursery, he had had it for so long he forgot his own name! Stinky had one question for life...

Hamdi Guled Guled Hasan (10)
Wood Farm Primary School, Headington

Flickering Lights

One rainy, cold day, there lived a girl called Ava, with her pet Spotty. They lived in an apartment. Ava started to get bored so she called over her friends to have a sleepover with her. Ava's friends arrived at her apartment. Then they started to play games and have pillow fights. They soon got tired. Ava started getting shivers down her spine because she felt something was following her. She started to go left and right to lose it but it kept following her. Then she realised it was just the flickering lights!

Nadine Da Silva (9)
Wood Farm Primary School, Headington

Hop The Burping Rabbit

Hop was a rabbit and he absolutely loved carrots. One day, whilst he was eating a mountain of carrots, he began burping. Burp! He was suddenly transported to the time of the dinosaurs. Burp! Now he was in the Stone-Age. Burp! Now he could hear Queen Victoria slurp up her tea. Burp! Now he was in WWI. Burp! He was in WWII. Burp! Finally he was back in his hutch. "Pardon me!" he said. He was exhausted and very tired. Hop took one last look at his carrots and decided he would never ever eat carrots again!

Stephana Sojan (9)
Wood Farm Primary School, Headington

Magical Ghost

One night, I was sleeping and I heard a door that was squeaking, that time I was scared! It was a magical ghost! I got out of bed and went to the door. The door was opening and closing. I was terrified. The next moment, I saw a light from the kitchen. The door stopped open. I could now have a good look! I did... He was making a blue electric light, it was an electric ball. I realised he was going to throw it at me. He missed and it went back at him.

Oliver Cupi (9)
Wood Farm Primary School, Headington

The Smelly Dino

Once upon a time, there was a little boy called David. He went out hunting one day when he saw something in the bushes. He decided to have a look and he spotted a green tail. It started to face him and he started to scream until this smelly thing showed its face. It said, "Please keep care of my baby, I need to go now but take of him!"
He did until he was old enough to get his prey. As he got older his mum decided to go see him.

Cody Davis (10)
Wood Farm Primary School, Headington

Evolution Of Pugs (Space Pugs 2)

They found a platypus in space. The pugs found an unknown creature. They took it to their home. There was a problem. Some of the pugs changed. The radiation in space made them weird and whacky. There was a pug with two heads and one eye. Another pug had eight legs! They had to make names for everyone. There was one pug who stayed normal. The pugs turned on him and made him leave the planet forever.

Lucas Brooks (9)
Wood Farm Primary School, Headington

YoungWriters®
— Est. 1991 —

YOUNG WRITERS
INFORMATION

We hope you have enjoyed reading this book – and that you will continue to in the coming years.

If you're a young writer who enjoys reading and creative writing, or the parent of an enthusiastic poet or story writer, do visit our website **www.youngwriters.co.uk**. Here you will find free competitions, workshops and games, as well as recommended reads, a poetry glossary and our blog. There's lots to keep budding writers motivated to write!

If you would like to order further copies of this book, or any of our other titles, then please give us a call or order via your online account.

Young Writers
Remus House
Coltsfoot Drive
Peterborough
PE2 9BF
(01733) 890066
info@youngwriters.co.uk

Join in the conversation!
Tips, news, giveaways and much more!

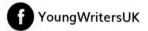 YoungWritersUK    @YoungWritersCW